P9-BZI-590

WRITTEN & ILLUSTRATED BY

HYPERION BOOKS FOR CHILDREN
NEW YORK

For information address Hyperion Books for Children, 114 Fifth Avenue,
New York, New York 10011-5690.
Printed in Hong Kong
First Edition
1 3 5 7 9 10 8 6 4 2
Library of Congress Cataloging-in-Publication Data on file.
Reinforced binding
ISBN-13: 978-1-4231-0173-4
ISBN-10: 1-4231-0173-1
Visit www.hyperionbooksforchildren.com

For Emily and Josh, always

Deep in the woods,
at the foot of a mountain,
lived a moose.
He had no family,
few friends,
and rarely entertained visitors.

He spent his days alone in the center
of the lake, like an island unto himself.

Early one evening,
Moose was out
gathering pond
weeds . . .

when he heard a strange fluttering sound,
followed by a *SPLASH!*

In front of him was a small
bird, clinging to
a lily pad.

Moose hesitated for a moment,
then tilted his head and
offered an antler.

Bird climbed on.

Moose waded ashore and gently shook his antlers.
“Hey, thanks for the ride!” said Bird.

Then, with great difficulty,
he flapped his wings . . .

rose several
feet into the air,

and then . . .

fell

straight

to the

ground!

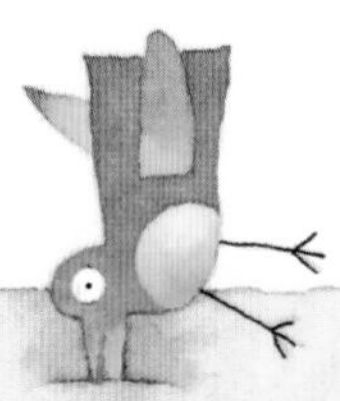

"Yikes!" moaned Bird.

“Yikes, indeed,” groaned Moose.

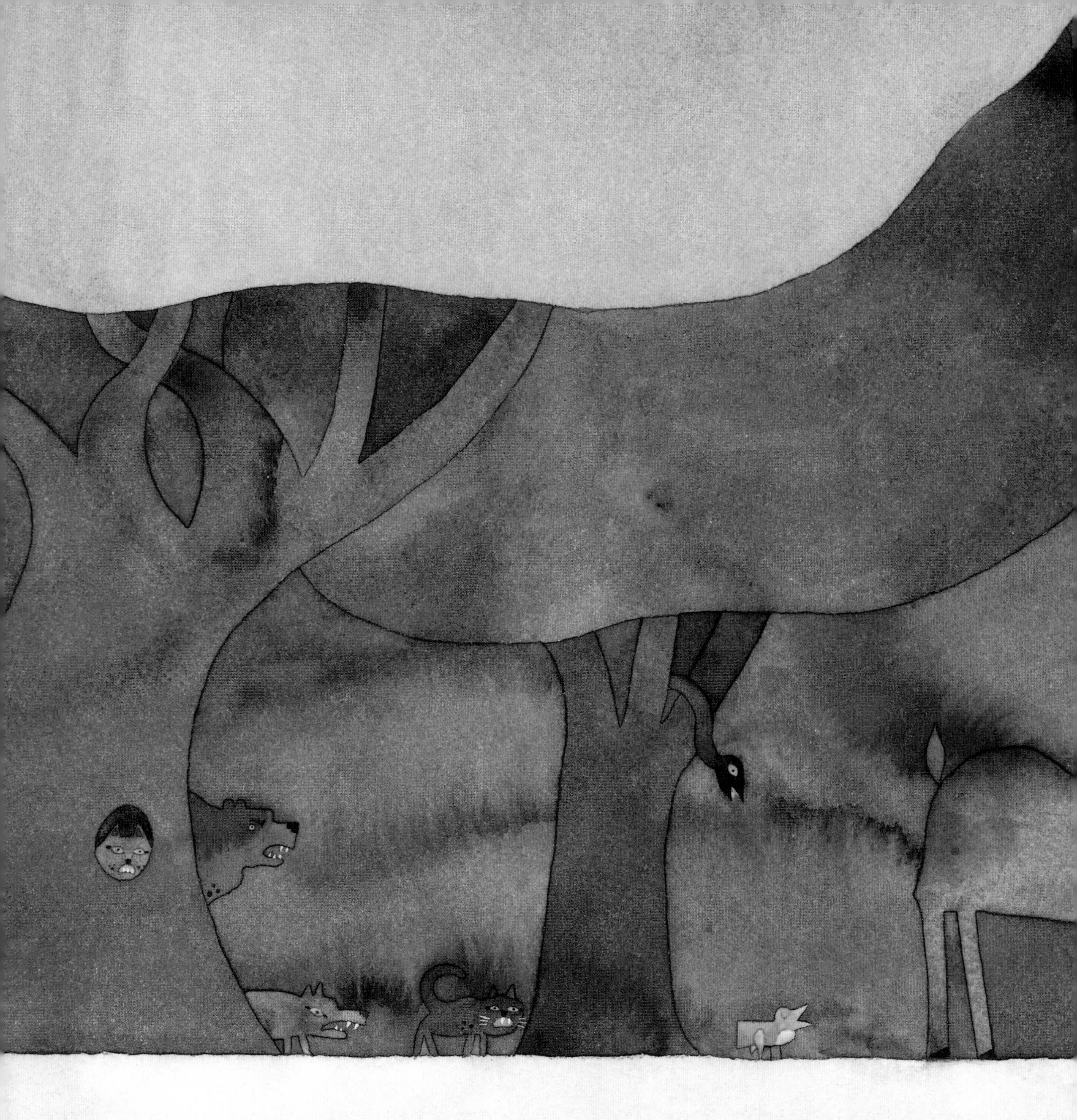

Night was falling.
The forest grew dark.

“This is no place for a bird that cannot fly,” said Moose.
“Bird, come. NOW!”

“My hero—you saved me!”

“QUIET,” said Moose.
“It’s late.”

Early the next morning,
Moose awoke to singing.

“Good morning!” chirped Bird.

“QUIET,” said Moose.
“It’s early.”

By afternoon, Bird was hungry.
They walked to the meadow to dig for worms.

"Try one," said Bird.
"They're delicious."

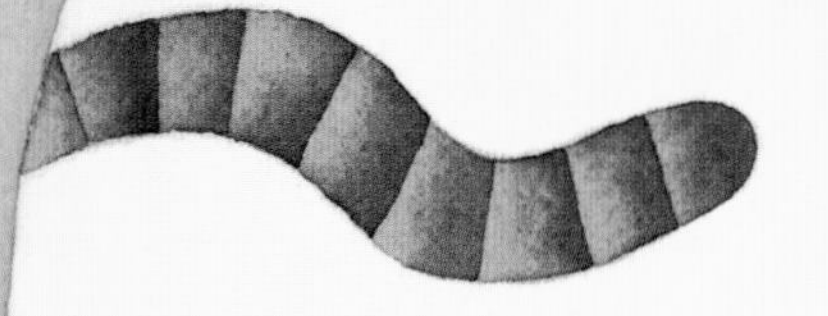

Moose tried one.

Revolting, he thought.

All summer long,
their days
were full.

Most mornings, Moose
and Bird picked berries
and gathered weeds.

In the afternoon, they
bathed in the lake.

Sometimes they climbed
to the top of the mountain,
just to enjoy the view.

Days became weeks . . .

and Bird still could not fly.

One morning, while out for a walk,
Moose and Bird smelled something. . . .

Smoke?

Fire!

The sky filled with
dark, bitter smoke.

Moose ran.
Bird fell.

"Bird! Bird!" cried Moose.

Bird nervously flapped
his wings.

He rose into the air,
paused, and then . . .

flew away to safety.

When the smoke cleared, Moose was alone.

Bird was gone.

The seasons changed. Summer turned to fall and fall into winter.

Winter became spring. Moose was sad.

"Where is Bird?" he wondered.

The weather grew warmer. Leaves appeared on the trees. Flowers bloomed. The forest was coming back to life.

Moose was at the pond gathering fresh pond weeds when he heard a familiar fluttering sound. . . .

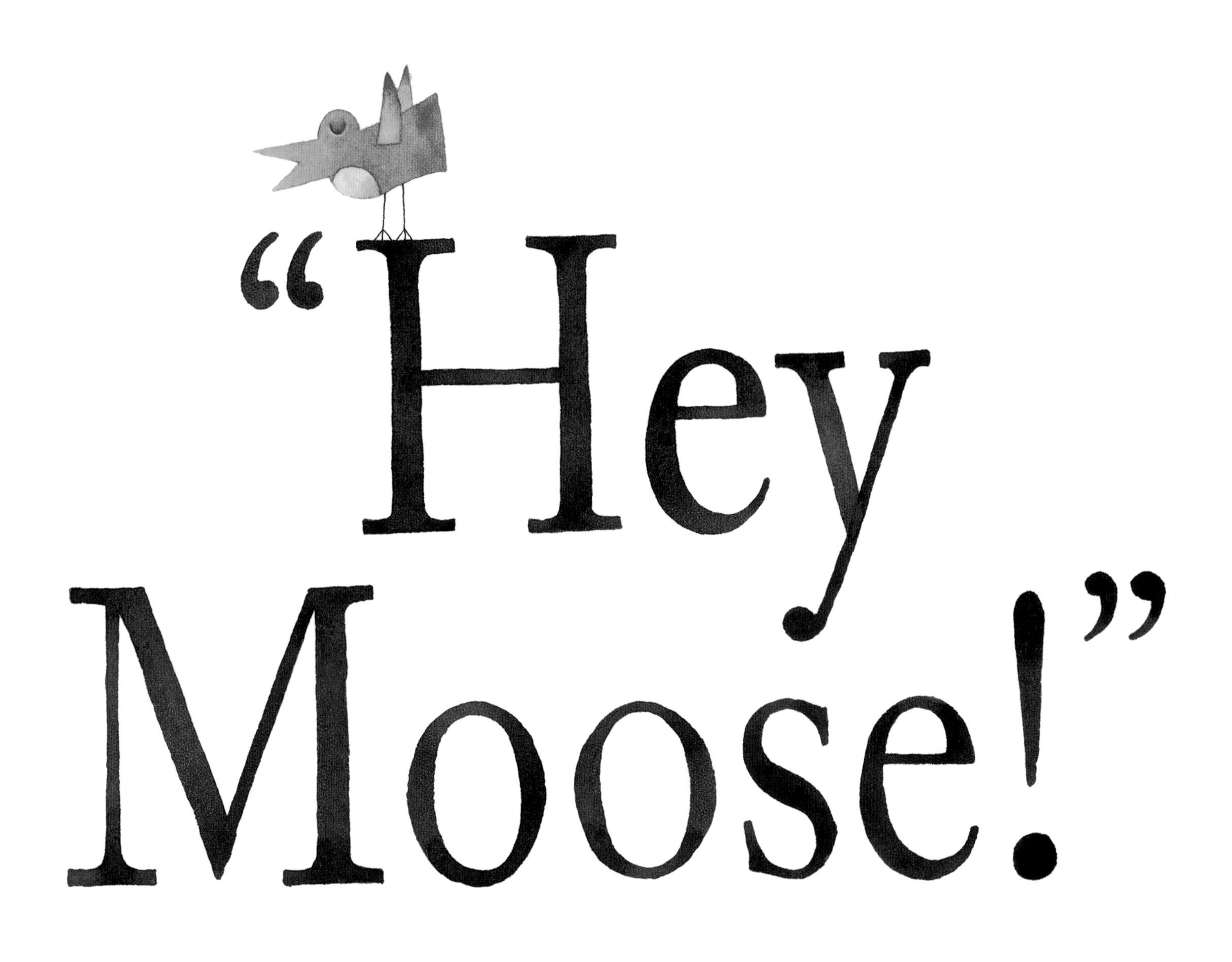
"Hey Moose!"

“Welcome home, Bird, I missed you.”

“I missed you too, Moose.”

"I brought some friends with me."

"FRIENDS?"

"Moose, you can never have too many friends!"